Black Sky River

by Tres Seymour • paintings by Dan Andreasen

Orchard Books • New York

Orchard Books, 95 Madison Avenue, New York, NY 10016

Manufactured in the United States of America. Printed by Barton Press, Inc.
Bound by Horowitz/Rae. Book design by Jean Krulis. The text of this book is
set in 16 point Bembo. The illustrations are oil on gessoed illustration board.

10   9   8   7   6   5   4   3   2   1

Library of Congress Cataloging-in-Publication Data. Seymour, Tres. Black sky
river / by Tres Seymour ; paintings by Dan Andreasen. p.   cm. "A Richard
Jackson book"—Half t.p. Summary: In its "old, old, old familiar way," an "endless ribbon" of birds, with its noise and germs, flies over a town, until the
townspeople decide to do something about it. ISBN 0-531-09537-1. — ISBN
0-531-08887-1 (lib. bdg.) [1. Birds—Migration—Fiction.   2. Man—Influence
on nature—Fiction.]   I. Andreasen, Dan, ill.   II. Title.   PZ7.S5253B54
1996   [E]—dc20   95-51564

To Clark

—T.S.

For my children,
Brett and Emily

—D.A.

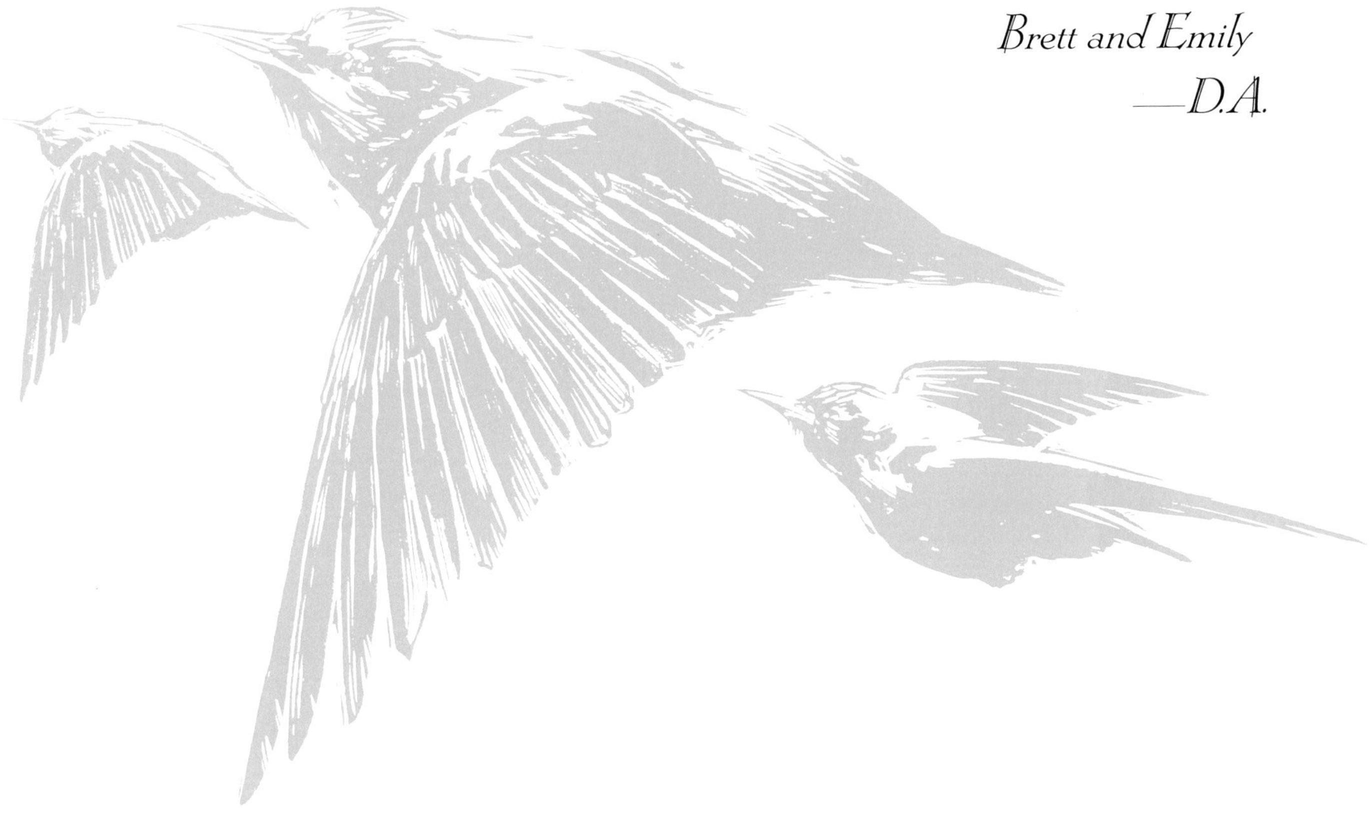

I used to sit,
as you sit now,
on Papaw's crooked white rail fence
and watch the Black Sky River flow.
A long, dark, endless ribbon
singing *FWEET! FWEET! FWEET! FWEET! CHACKLE!*
CHACKLE! CHAK!
as it flew its old, old, old familiar way.

I tried to count them
once,
but I didn't know what came after
thousands.

I never saw the River start;
I never saw it end.

At dusk the Black Sky River settled down
like dew
into the trees to roost,
singing *FWEET! FWEET! FWEET! FWEET! CHACKLE!*
CHACKLE! CHAK!
all night long.

At dawn
the birds were gone.
But they had kept the neighborhood awake
and painted the statue in the square that's stood there
since the Civil War,
painted it in spots of white and gray.

"The noise!" everybody said.
"The germs!" said everyone.

So they scattered bitter seed to feed the birds.

I never saw the Black Sky River start;
I never saw it end

until one day.

The bitter seed had done its work.

The River shrank to little flocks
that rushed across the sky.
They still remembered where to go
but did not flow like water.

I tried to count them
once.
I could count a hundred.

I sat on Papaw's crooked white rail fence
looking always for the Black Sky River,
listening for the *FWEET! FWEET! FWEET! FWEET! CHACKLE!*
CHACKLE! CHAK!

I miss the mystery, the wondering
of things without beginning, without end.

Someday you and I will find a place
with trees and fields and no bad seed.
We'll sit on our own crooked white rail fence
and watch
and hope to see...

the Black Sky River flow again.

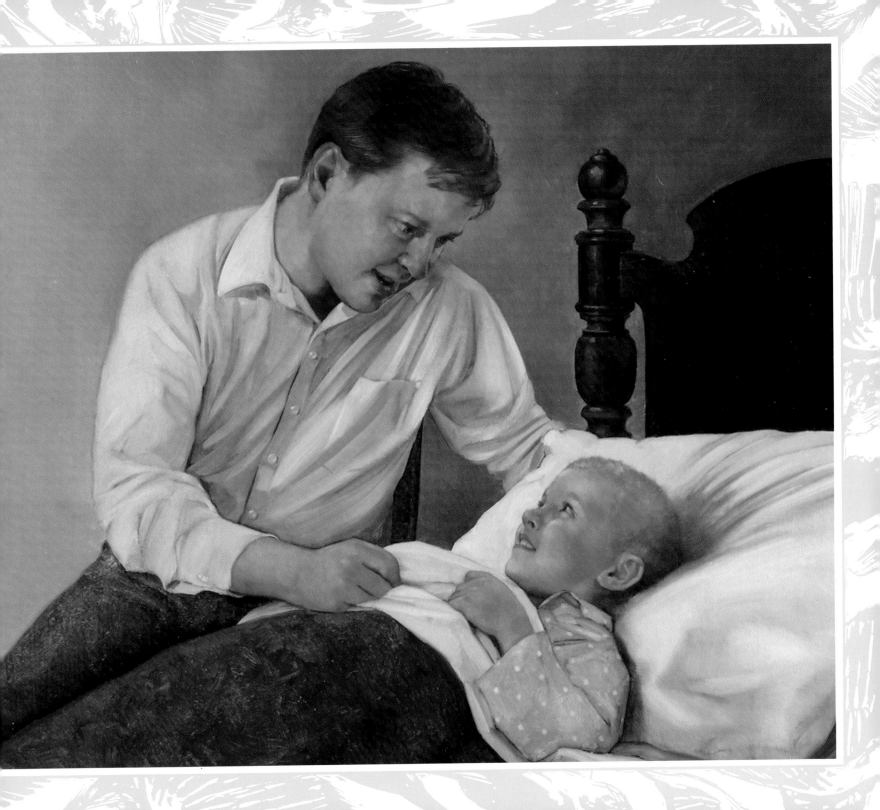